CONFIDENTIAL

DIARY 1987

Two-Can Design

Published by
Two-Can Design Ltd
27 Cowper Street
London EC2A 4AP

in association with
BBC Publications
35 Marylebone High Street
London W1M 9AA

Edited by Diane James and Jean Beith
Handwriting by James Partridge
Typeset by Impact Origination
Printed in Great Britain
by Blantyre Printing & Binding Co. Limited
ISBN 0 563 20541 5

H.

Macte nova virtute puer; sic itur ad astra.

or, as Shakespeare said —

"Thou has it now: King, Cawdor,

Glanis, all."

A.

NOTABLE DATES

New Year's Holiday (UK and Rep. of Ireland)	January 1
Bank Holiday (Scotland)	January 2
Australia Day	January 26
Waitangi Day (New Zealand)	February 6
St. Valentine's Day	February 14
St. David's Day	March 1
Shrove Tuesday	March 3
Ash Wednesday	March 4
Canberra Day	March 16
St. Patrick's Day (N. Ireland and Rep. of Ireland)	March 17
Spring begins	March 21
Mothering Sunday	March 29
Festival of Passover (Pesach)	April 14
Good Friday	April 17
Easter Sunday	April 19
Easter Monday Bank Holiday in UK (except Scotland)	April 20
St. George's Day	April 23
Anzac Day	April 25
Anzac Day Holiday	April 27
Ramadan 1st day of	April 30
Bank Holiday in UK	May 4
Late Spring Bank Holiday in UK	May 25
Ascension Day	May 28
Queen's Birthday (New Zealand)	June 1
Queen's Birthday (Australia)	June 8
Corpus Christi	June 18
Father's Day (GB and USA)	June 21
Summer begins, longest day	June 21
Battle of the Boyne Holiday (N. Ireland)	July 13
St. Swithin's Day	July 15
Bank Holiday (Scotland and Rep. of Ireland)	August 3
Late Summer Holiday (England, N. Ireland, Wales)	August 31
Autumn begins	September 23
Jewish New Year AM 5748 (Rosh Hashanah)	September 24
Day of Atonement (Yom Kippur)	October 3
Succoth 1st Day	October 8
Labor Day (New Zealand)	October 26
Melbourne Cup Day	November 3
Remembrance Sunday	November 8
St. Andrew's Day	November 30
Winter begins, shortest day	December 22
Christmas Day (Friday)	December 25
Bank Holiday in UK	December 28
New Year's Eve (Hogmanay)	December 31

NOTABLE EVENTS

Jan. 9 International Boat Show, Earls Court
Jan. 15-Apr. 5 British Art in the 20th Century, Royal Academy
Jan. 17 International Rugby, Twickenham (England v Scotland)
Feb. 21 International Rugby, Twickenham (England v France)
Mar. 5-Jun. 7 Le Corbusier Exhibition, Hayward Gallery
Mar. 9-Apr. 5 Ideal Home Exhibition, Earls Court
Mar. 17-19 Cheltenham Gold Cup
Apr. 4 Grand National, Aintree
Apr. 9-12 Badminton Horse Trials
Apr. 18 Oxford v Cambridge Boat Race
Apr. 25 John Player Cup Final, Twickenham
May 16 F.A. Cup Final, Wembley
May 19-22 Chelsea Flower Show
May 25-Aug. 15 Glyndebourne season
Jun. 3 Derby Day, Epsom
Jun. 13 Trooping the Colour
Jun. 16-20 Royal Ascot
Jun. 20 2nd Cornhill Test v Pakistan, Lords
Jun. 22-Jul 5 All England Tennis Championship, Wimbledon
Jul. 1-5 Henley Regatta
Jul. 5 Men's Final, Wimbledon
Jul. 11 Benson and Hedges Final, Lords
Jul. 15-25 City of London Festival
Jul. 16-19 British Open Golf Championships
Jul. 17-Sept. 12 Promenade Concerts, Albert Hall
Aug. 8 5th Cornhill Test v Pakistan, Oval
Aug. 9-29 Edinburgh Festival
Sept. 5 Nat-West Final, Lords
Sept. 12 Last night of the Proms, Albert Hall
Oct. 1 The Age of Hogarth Exhibition, Tate Gallery
Nov. 8 Remembrance Sunday
Dec. 8 Oxford v Cambridge, Twickenham

NOTES

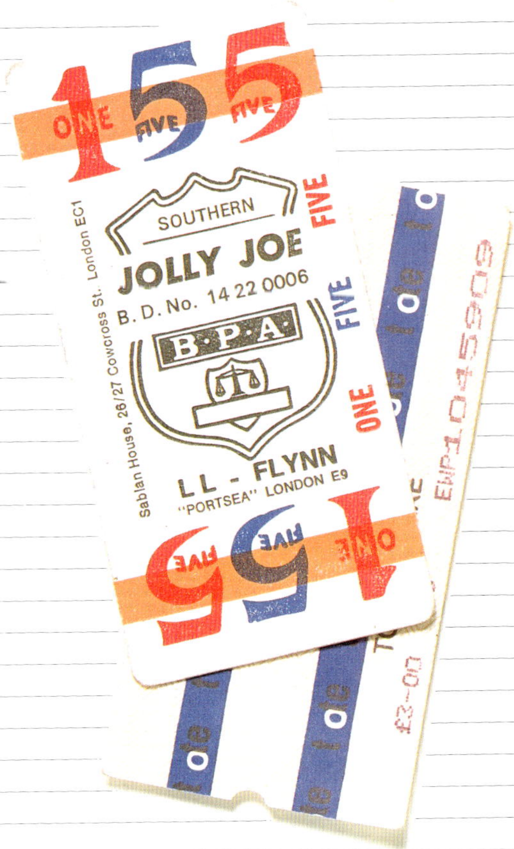

155
ONE
FIVE
FIVE
SOUTHERN
JOLLY JOE
B. D. No. 14 22 0006
B·P·A
LL - FLYNN
"PORTSEA" LONDON E9
Sablan House, 26/27 Cowcross St. London EC1
£3-00

YEAR PLANNER 1987

JAN	FEB	MAR	APR	MAY	JUN
T 1	S 1	S 1	W 1	F 1	M 1
F 2	M 2	M 2	T 2	S 2	T 2
S 3	T 3	T 3	F 3	S 3	W 3
S 4	W 4	W 4	S 4	M 4	T 4
M 5	T 5	T 5	S 5	T 5	F 5
T 6	F 6	F 6	M 6	W 6	S 6
W 7	S 7	S 7	T 7	T 7	S 7
T 8	S 8	S 8	W 8	F 8	M 8
F 9	M 9	M 9	T 9	S 9	T 9
S 10	T 10	T 10	F 10	S 10	W 10
S 11	W 11	W 11	S 11	M 11	T 11
M 12	T 12	T 12	S 12	T 12	F 12
T 13	F 13	F 13	M 13	W 13	S 13
W 14	S 14	S 14	T 14	T 14	S 14
T 15	S 15	S 15	W 15	F 15	M 15
F 16	M 16	M 16	T 16	S 16	Ascot. T 16
S 17	T 17	Cheltenham? T 17	F 17	S 17	W 17
S 18	W 18	W 18	S 18	M 18	T 18
M 19	T 19	T 19	S 19	T 19	Lord's? F 19
T 20	F 20	F 20	M 20	W 20	S 20
W 21	S 21	S 21	T 21	T 21	S 21
T 22	S 22	S 22	W 22	F 22	M 22
F 23	M 23	M 23	T 23	S 23	T 23
S 24	T 24	T 24	F 24	S 24	W 24
S 25	W 25	W 25	S 25	M 25 Glyndebourne.	T 25
M 26	T 26	T 26	S 26	T 26	F 26
T 27	F 27	F 27	M 27	W 27	S 27
W 28	S 28	S 28	T 28	T 28	S 28
T 29		S 29	W 29	F 29	M 29
F 30		M 30	T 30	S 30	T 30
S 31		T 31		S 31	

YEAR PLANNER 1987

JUL	AUG	SEP	OCT	NOV	DEC
W 1	S 1	T 1	T 1	S 1	T 1
T 2	S 2	W 2	F 2	M 2	W 2
F 3	M 3	T 3	S 3	T 3	T 3
S 4	T 4	F 4	S 4	W 4	F 4
S 5	W 5	S 5	M 5	T 5	S 5
M 6	T 6	S 6	T 6	F 6	S 6
T 7	F 7	M 7	W 7	S 7	M 7
W 8	S 8	T 8	T 8	S 8	T 8
T 9	S 9	W 9	F 9	M 9	W 9
F 10	Holiday M 10	T 10	S 10	T 10	T 10
S 11	T 11	F 11	S 11	W 11	F 11
S 12	W 12	S 12	M 12	T 12	S 12
M 13	T 13	S 13	T 13	F 13	S 13
T 14	F 14	M 14	W 14	S 14	M 14
W 15	S 15	T 15	T 15	S 15	T 15
T 16	S 16	W 16	F 16	M 16	W 16
Proms. F 17	M 17	T 17	S 17	T 17	T 17
S 18	T 18	F 18	S 18	W 18	F 18
S 19	W 19	S 19	M 19	T 19	S 19
M 20	T 20	S 20	T 20	F 20	S 20
T 21	F 21	M 21	W 21	S 21	M 21
W 22	S 22	T 22	T 22	S 22	T 22
T 23	S 23	W 23	F 23	M 23	W 23
F 24	M 24	T 24	S 24	T 24	T 24
S 25	T 25	F 25	S 25	W 25	F 25
S 26	W 26	S 26	M 26	T 26	S 26
M 27	T 27	S 27	T 27	F 27	S 27
T 28	F 28	M 28	W 28	S 28	M 28
W 29	S 29	T 29	T 29	S 29	T 29
T 30	S 30	wedding anniversary. W 30	F 30	M 30	W 30
F 31	M 31		S 31		T 31

DECEMBER 1986/JANUARY 1987

MONDAY 29
(363-2) WEEK 1

It's no good saying something is common sense. Government policy has nothing to do with common sense.

TUESDAY 30
(364-1) WEEK 1

WEDNESDAY 31
(365) WEEK 1
● New Moon

THURSDAY 1
(1-364) WEEK 1
New Year's Day—Bank Holiday in UK, Republic of Ireland, Canada & USA

JANUARY

FRIDAY 2

(2-363) WEEK 1
Bank Holiday in Scotland

SATURDAY 3

(3-362) WEEK 1
sr 08.06, ss 16.04

Basic Ministerial skills:

1) Blurring issues
2) Delaying decisions
3) Dodging questions
4) Juggling figures
5) Bending facts
6) Concealing errors.

SUNDAY 4

(4-361) WEEK 1
2nd after Christmas
PAYE Week 40

JANUARY

MONDAY 5
(5-360) WEEK 2

The Foreign Office never expect the Cabinet to agree to any of their policies. That's why they never fully explain them.

TUESDAY 6
(6-359) WEEK 2
◐ First Quarter Epiphany

WEDNESDAY 7
(7-358) WEEK 2

Open government is a contradiction in terms. You can be open, or you can have government.

THURSDAY 8
(8-357) WEEK 2

JANUARY

FRIDAY **9**
(9-356) WEEK 2

SATURDAY **10**
(10-355) WEEK 2
sr 08.04, ss 16.13

The citizens of a democracy have a right to be ignorant. Knowledge only means complicity and guilt. Ignorance has a certain dignity.

SUNDAY **11**
(11-354) WEEK 2
1st after Epiphany
PAYE Week 41

JANUARY

MONDAY **12**
(12-353) WEEK 3

TUESDAY **13**
(13-352) WEEK 3

WEDNESDAY **14**
(14-351) WEEK 3

Politicians are more leaked against
than leaking.

THURSDAY **15**
(15-350) WEEK 3
○ Full Moon

FRIDAY 16
(16-349) WEEK 3

The Foreign Office is pro-Europe because it is really anti-Europe. In fact the Civil Service was united in its desire to make sure the Common Market didn't work. That's why we went into it.

SATURDAY 17
(17-348) WEEK 3
sr 07.58, ss 16.23

SUNDAY 18
(18-347) WEEK 3
2nd after Epiphany
PAYE Week 42

JANUARY

MONDAY **19**
(19-346) WEEK 4
Martin Luther King Day

TUESDAY **20**
(20-345) WEEK 4

The Queen is inseparable from the Church of England. I think God is what is called an optional extra.

WEDNESDAY **21**
(21-344) WEEK 4

THURSDAY **22**
(22-343) WEEK 4
◑ Last Quarter

With the administration of the EEC in Brussels and the Parliament in Strasbourg, it's like having London as the capital with the House of Commons in Swindon and the Civil Service in Kettering.

FRIDAY 23
(23-342) WEEK 4

The government is not a team – it's a loose confederation of warring tribes.

SATURDAY 24
(24-341) WEEK 4
sr 07.51, ss 16.35

SUNDAY 25
(25-340) WEEK 4
3rd after Epiphany
PAYE Week 43

JANUARY

MONDAY

26

(26-339) WEEK 5
Australia Day

TUESDAY

27

(27-338) WEEK 5

WEDNESDAY

28

(28-337) WEEK 5

THURSDAY

29

(29-336) WEEK 5
● New Moon

It is axiomatic with Civil Servants that information should only be revealed to their political 'masters' when absolutely necessary, and to the public when absolutely unavoidable.

FRIDAY 30

(30-335) WEEK 5

SATURDAY 31

(31-334) WEEK 5

sr 07.41, ss 16.47

We should always tell the press, freely and frankly, anything that they can easily find out some other way.

SUNDAY 1

(32-333) WEEK 5

4th after Epiphany

PAYE Week 44

FEBRUARY

MONDAY
(33-332) WEEK 6

2

The EEC is just like the United Nations. The more members it has, the more arguments you can stir up, and the more futile and impotent it becomes.

TUESDAY
(34-331) WEEK 6

3

WEDNESDAY
(35-330) WEEK 6

4

The Civil Service when drafting a Minister's speech is primarily concerned with making him nail his trousers to the mast. Then he can't climb down!

THURSDAY
(36-329) WEEK 6

◐ First Quarter

5

FRIDAY **6**
(37-328) WEEK 6
Accession of Queen Elizabeth II
Waitangi Day (New Zealand)

SATURDAY **7**
(38-327) WEEK 6
sr 07.30, ss 17.00

A cover-up is merely a responsible decision exercised in the national interest to prevent unnecessary disclosure of eminently justifiable procedures in which untimely revelation would severely impair public confidence.

SUNDAY **8**
(39-326) WEEK 6
5th after Epiphany
PAYE Week 45

Prime Ministers have little choice in forming governments. There are only 630 MPs and a party with just over 300 MPs forms a Government – and of these 300, 100 are too old and silly to be Ministers and 100 too young and too callow. Therefore there are about 100 MPs to fill 100 Government posts. Effectively no choice at all.

FEBRUARY

MONDAY 9
(40-325) WEEK 7

TUESDAY 10
(41-324) WEEK 7

In ten years the number of Health Service administrators has gone up by 40,000 and the number of hospital beds has gone down by 60,000. These figures speak for themselves.

WEDNESDAY 11
(42-323) WEEK 7

THURSDAY 12
(43-322) WEEK 7

FRIDAY **13**
(44-321) WEEK 7
○ Full Moon

SATURDAY **14**
(45-320) WEEK 7
St. Valentine's Day
sr 07.18, ss 17.13

Once you allow Ministers to write draft reports, the next thing you know they'll be dictating Government policy.

SUNDAY **15**
(46-319) WEEK 7
Septuagesima
PAYE Week 46

FEBRUARY

MONDAY **16**
(47-318) WEEK 8
Washington's Birthday Observance

To block Civil Servants' honours until they had achieved economics would create a very dangerous precedent.

TUESDAY **17**
(48-317) WEEK 8

WEDNESDAY **18**
(49-316) WEEK 8

THURSDAY **19**
(50-315) WEEK 8

Ministers are always vulnerable when they are in a hurry. That is why we always keep them busy.

FEBRUARY

FRIDAY **20**
(51-314) WEEK 8

SATURDAY **21**
(52 313) WEEK 8
◑ Last Quarter
sr 07.04, ss 17.26

SUNDAY **22**
(53-312) WEEK 8
Sexagesima
PAYE Week 47

<u>Functions of a Minister</u>

(1) He is an advocate. He makes the Department's actions seem plausible to Parliament and the public.
(2) He is our man in Westminster, steering our legislation through Parliament (NB: <u>ours</u> not his).
(3) He is our Breadwinner. His duty is to fight in Cabinet for the money we need to do our job.

FEBRUARY

MONDAY **23**
(54-311) WEEK 9

TUESDAY **24**
(55-310) WEEK 9

The Comprehensive School Excuse: It's only gone wrong because of heavy cuts in staff and budget which have stretched supervisory resources beyond the limit.

WEDNESDAY **25**
(56-309) WEEK 9

THURSDAY **26**
(57-308) WEEK 9

FRIDAY **27**
(58-307) WEEK 9

SATURDAY **28**
(59-306) WEEK 9
● New Moon
sr 06.49, ss 17.38

The Charge of the Light Brigade Excuse: It was an unfortunate lapse by an individual which has been dealt with under internal disciplinary procedures.

SUNDAY **1**
(60-305) WEEK 9
St. David's Day Quinquagesima
PAYE Week 48

MARCH

MONDAY
(61-304) WEEK 10

2

TUESDAY
(62-303) WEEK 10
Shrove Tuesday

3

WEDNESDAY
(63-302) WEEK 10
Ash Wednesday

4

Ministers are not experts.
Ministers are put in charge
precisely because they know
nothing.

THURSDAY
(64-301) WEEK 10

5

FRIDAY **6**
(65-300) WEEK 10

The Treasury was rather more competent before the invention of the xerox than it is now, because its officials had so much less to read.

SATURDAY **7**
(66-299) WEEK 10
◐ First Quarter
sr 06.34, ss 17.51

SUNDAY **8**
(67-298) WEEK 10
1st Sunday in Lent
PAYE Week 49

The Munich Agreement Excuse: It occurred before important facts were known, and cannot happen again.

Note on Ministers moving to the House of Lords: Approbation, elevation and castration, all in one stroke.

MARCH

MONDAY **9**
(68-297) WEEK 11

The Anthony Blunt Excuse: There is a perfectly satisfactory explanation for everything, but security prevents its disclosure.

TUESDAY **10**
(69-296) WEEK 11

WEDNESDAY **11**
(70-295) WEEK 11

THURSDAY **12**
(71-294) WEEK 11

FRIDAY **13**
(72-293) WEEK 11

SATURDAY **14**
(73-292) WEEK 11
sr 06.18, ss 18.03

The Concorde Excuse: It was a worthwhile experiment now abandoned but not before it provided much valuable data and considerable employment.

SUNDAY **15**
(74-291) WEEK 11
○ Full Moon 2nd Sunday in Lent
PAYE Week 50

MARCH

MONDAY 16
(75-290) WEEK 12
Canberra Day

Press statements aren't delivered under oath.

TUESDAY 17
(76-289) WEEK 12
St. Patrick's Day—Bank Holiday in N. Ireland & Rep. of Ireland

WEDNESDAY 18
(77-288) WEEK 12

THURSDAY 19
(78-287) WEEK 12

You are ideally qualified to be a Minister if you can deliver activity, but no actual achievement. Ministers need activity as their substitute for achievement.

FRIDAY **20**
(79-286) WEEK 12

SATURDAY **21**
(80-285) WEEK 12
sr 06.03, ss 18.14

Bishops tend to have long lives – apparently the Lord isn't all that keen for them to join him!

SUNDAY **22**
(81-284) WEEK 12
◑ Last Quarter 3rd Sunday in Lent
PAYE Week 51

Good Chap Theory: A Good Chap Does Not Tell a Good Chap What a Good Chap Ought To Know.

MARCH

MONDAY 23
(82-283) WEEK 13

TUESDAY 24
(83-282) WEEK 13

House-trained: Civil Service phrase for making a new Prime Minister see things our way.

WEDNESDAY 25
(84-281) WEEK 13

THURSDAY 26
(85-280) WEEK 13

FRIDAY **27**
(86-279) WEEK 13

The part we offer to Ministers:
If the Minister will help us implement the opposite policy to the one to which he is pledged, we will help him to pretend that he is in fact doing what he said he was going to do in his manifesto.

SATURDAY **28**
(87-278) WEEK 13
sr 05.47, ss 18.26

SUNDAY **29**
(88-277) WEEK 13
● New Moon 4th Sunday in Lent Mothering Sunday
British Summertime begins PAYE Week 52

We are here to see that the Prime Minister is not confused. Politicians are simple people. They like simple choices. Clear guidance. They don't like doubt and conflict. They get quite enough of that in the ~~zoo~~ House of Commons.

Government is about principle. And the principle is don't rock the boat. Because if you do rock the boat all the little consciences fall out.

MARCH/APRIL

MONDAY 30
(89-276) WEEK 14

Ministers, unlike Civil Servants, are selected completely at random – by Prime Ministerial whim, in recognition of doubtful favours received or to avoid appointing someone of real ability who might become a threat.

TUESDAY 31
(90-275) WEEK 14

WEDNESDAY 1
(91-274) WEEK 14

As a matter of principle, Ministers should never know more than they need to know. Just like secret agents. They may be captured and tortured by the BBC, for example.

THURSDAY 2
(92-273) WEEK 14

APRIL

FRIDAY 3
(93-272) WEEK 14

SATURDAY 4
(94-271) WEEK 14
sr 06.31, ss 19.38

SUNDAY 5
(95-270) WEEK 14
5th Sunday in Lent

This is an urgent problem and we therefore propose setting up a Royal Commission. Civil Service Meaning: The problem is a bloody nuisance, but we hope that by the time a Royal Commission reports, four years from now, everyone will have forgotten about it or we can find someone else to blame.

APRIL

MONDAY 6
(96-269) WEEK 15
◐ First Quarter
PAYE Week 1

TUESDAY 7
(97-268) WEEK 15

WEDNESDAY 8
(98-267) WEEK 15

Opposition is about asking
awkward questions and
government is about not
answering them.

THURSDAY 9
(99-266) WEEK 15

APRIL

FRIDAY **10**
(100-265) WEEK 15

We do not mind whether the Minister is re-elected or not. As far as this Department is concerned, it makes very little difference who the Minister is.

SATURDAY **11**
(101-264) WEEK 15
sr 06.15, ss 19.50

SUNDAY **12**
(102-263) WEEK 15
Palm Sunday

Giving powers of decision to the Civil Service helps to take government out of politics. That is Britain's only hope of survival.

A phased reduction of about a hundred thousand people is not in the public interest.
Civil Service Meaning: It is in the public interest but it is not in the interest of the Civil Service.

APRIL

MONDAY 13
(103-262) WEEK 16
PAYE Week 2

TUESDAY 14
(104-261) WEEK 16
○ Full Moon

There are grave problems about circulating papers before they are written.

WEDNESDAY 15
(105-260) WEEK 16

THURSDAY 16
(106-259) WEEK 16

APRIL

FRIDAY **17**
(107-258) WEEK 16
Good Friday

SATURDAY **18**
(108-257) WEEK 16
sr 06.00, ss 20.01

SUNDAY **19**
(109-256) WEEK 16
Easter Day

Three Varieties of Civil Service Silence:

(1) Discreet silence: the silence when we do not want to tell them the facts.
(2) Stubborn silence: the silence when we do not intend to take any action.
(3) Courageous silence: the silence when they catch us out and we haven't got a leg to stand on. We imply that we could vindicate ourselves completely if only we were free to tell all, but we are too honourable to do so.

APRIL

MONDAY 20

(110-255) WEEK 17

◑ Last Quarter Bank Holiday in UK, (except Scotland), Rep. of Ireland & Canada PAYE Week 3

The main reason why it's too dangerous to publish the results of an enquiry is because most leaks come from Number 10.
The ship of state is the only vessel that leaks from the top!

TUESDAY 21

(111-254) WEEK 17

Birthday of Queen Elizabeth II

Diplomacy is about surviving till the next century. Politics is about surviving till Friday afternoon.

WEDNESDAY 22

(112-253) WEEK 17

THURSDAY 23

(113-252) WEEK 17

St. George's Day

FRIDAY **24**
(114-251) WEEK 17

SATURDAY **25**
(115-250) WEEK 17
sr 05.45, ss 20.13
Anzac Day

SUNDAY **26**
(116-249) WEEK 17
Low Sunday

When the chips are down and the balloon goes up and the lights go out... there has to be somewhere to carry on Government, even if everything else stops. Government doesn't stop merely because the country's been destroyed.

APRIL

MONDAY **27**
(117-248) WEEK 18
PAYE Week 4
Anzac Day holiday

TUESDAY **28**
(118-247) WEEK 18
● New Moon

Government buildings do not need fire safety clearance. Presumably because Her Majesty's Civil Servants are not easily inflamed.

WEDNESDAY **29**
(119-246) WEEK 18

THURSDAY **30**
(120-245) WEEK 18

FRIDAY **1**
(121-244) WEEK 18

Politicians should be too busy to draft any documents themselves. And he who drafts the document wins the day.

SATURDAY **2**
(122-243) WEEK 18
sr 05.32, ss 20.25

If we wish to drop the whole scheme, recommend: (1) a pause to regroup, (2) a lull in which we reassess the position and discuss alternative strategies, (3) a space of time for mature reflection and deliberation.

SUNDAY **3**
(123-242) WEEK 18
2nd after Easter

MAY

MONDAY 4
(124-241) WEEK 19
Bank Holiday in UK
PAYE Week 5

TUESDAY 5
(125-240) WEEK 19

WEDNESDAY 6
(126-239) WEEK 19
◐ First Quarter

The UN is the accepted forum for the expression of international hatred.

THURSDAY 7
(127-238) WEEK 19

FRIDAY **8**
(128-237) WEEK 19

SATURDAY **9**
(129-236) WEEK 19
sr 05.19, ss 20.36

SUNDAY **10**
(130-235) WEEK 19
3rd after Easter
Mother's Day, USA & Canada

The term Underdeveloped Countries was considered offensive. So they called them Developing Countries. This term apparently was patronising. Then they became Less Developed Countries or LDCs, for short. The term Less Developed Countries is not yet causing offence to anyone. When it does, we are immediately to replace the term LDCs with HRRCs. This is short for Human Resource-Rich Countries. In other words they are grossly overpopulated and begging for money.

MAY

MONDAY 11
(131-234) WEEK 20
PAYE Week 6

MPs are not chosen by the people – they are chosen by their local constituency party, ie. thirty-five men in grubby raincoats or thirty-five women in silly hats.

TUESDAY 12
(132-233) WEEK 20

WEDNESDAY 13
(133-232) WEEK 20
O Full Moon

THURSDAY 14
(134-231) WEEK 20

Whitehall is the most secretive square mile in the world. The great emphasis on avoidance of error also means that avoidance of publication is equally necessary.

FRIDAY **15**
(135-230) WEEK 20

SATURDAY **16**
(136-229) WEEK 20
sr 05.08, ss 20.47

The Hot Line to Russia is not tested too often. It tends to create unnecessary panic at the other end. And panic is a good thing to avoid where nuclear weapons are concerned.

SUNDAY **17**
(137-228) WEEK 20
4th after Easter

MAY

MONDAY

18

(138-227) WEEK 21
Bank Holiday in Canada
PAYE Week 7

TUESDAY

19

(139-226) WEEK 21

WEDNESDAY

20

(140-225) WEEK 21
◑ Last Quarter

If Ministers need to know anything it will be brought to their attention. If they go out looking for information they might find it.

THURSDAY

21

(141-224) WEEK 21

FRIDAY **22**
(142-223) WEEK 21

You do not open a national debate until the government has privately made up its mind.

SATURDAY **23**
(143-222) WEEK 21
sr 04.59, ss 20.57

A decision is a decision only if it is the decision you wanted. Otherwise, it is merely the course the Minister seems to favour at the moment.

SUNDAY **24**
(144-221) WEEK 21
Rogation Sunday

MAY

MONDAY 25

(145-220) WEEK 22
Bank Holiday in UK & USA
PAYE Week 8

The Civil Service merely exists to implement legislation that is enacted by Parliament. So long as Parliament continues to legislate for more and more control over people's lives, the Civil Service must grow.

TUESDAY 26

(146-219) WEEK 22

WEDNESDAY 27

(147-218) WEEK 22
● New Moon

It's safer to be heartless than mindless. The history of the world is the history of the triumph of the heartless over the mindless.

THURSDAY 28

(148-217) WEEK 22
Ascension Day

FRIDAY **29**
(149-216) WEEK 22

SATURDAY **30**
(150-215) WEEK 22
sr 04.51, ss 21.06

SUNDAY **31**
(151-214) WEEK 22
Sunday after Ascension

Delaying phrases:
(1) The subject is still under discussion.
(2) The programme is not yet finalised.
(3) Nothing precipitate should be done.
(4) Failing instructions to the contrary, I propose that we await developments.

JUNE

MONDAY 1
(152-213) WEEK 23
Queen's Birthday (New Zealand)
PAYE Week 9

TUESDAY 2
(153-212) WEEK 23

WEDNESDAY 3
(154-211) WEEK 23

THURSDAY 4
(155-210) WEEK 23
◐ First Quarter

It is interesting that nowadays politicians want to talk about morals and bishops want to talk about politics.

FRIDAY 5
(156-209) WEEK 23

SATURDAY 6
(157-208) WEEK 23
sr 04.46, ss 21.13

Prime Ministers have had no proper selection or training, so it is our patriotic duty to arrange for them to make the right decisions as often as possible.

SUNDAY 7
(158-207) WEEK 23
Whit Sunday

Benefits of Ministerial absence: A Minister's absence is desirable because it enables you to do the job properly. There will be no:
(1) silly questions,
(2) bright ideas,
(3) fussing about what the papers are saying.

JUNE

MONDAY 8
(159-206) WEEK 24
PAYE Week 10
Queen's Birthday (Australia)

TUESDAY 9
(160-205) WEEK 24

It is not for Civil Servants to decide whether government policy is right or wrong. Almost all government policy is wrong, but frightfully well carried out.

WEDNESDAY 10
(161-204) WEEK 24

THURSDAY 11
(162-203) WEEK 24
○ Full Moon

An atheist clergyman couldn't continue to draw his stipend. So when they stop believing in God they call themselves modernists.

FRIDAY **12**
(163-202) WEEK 24

SATURDAY **13**
(164-201) WEEK 24
The Queen's Official Birthday
sr 04.43, ss 21.18

Clearly we cannot have Arts money going to support popular sports. It's just subsidising self-indulgence.

SUNDAY **14**
(165-200) WEEK 24
Trinity Sunday

JUNE

MONDAY 15
(166-199) WEEK 25
PAYE Week 11

Civil Servants are grown like oak trees, not mustard and cress. They bloom and ripen with the seasons. They mature like an old port.

TUESDAY 16
(167-198) WEEK 25

WEDNESDAY 17
(168-197) WEEK 25

THURSDAY 18
(169-196) WEEK 25
◑ Last Quarter

FRIDAY **19**
(170-195) WEEK 25

We are calling the White Paper Open Government because you always dispose of the difficult bit in the title. It does less harm there than on the statute books.

SATURDAY **20**
(171-194) WEEK 25
sr 04.43, ss 21.21

SUNDAY **21**
(172-193) WEEK 25
1st after Trinity
Longest Day — Father's Day

Facts complicate things. All that the press, the people and their elected leaders want to know is who are the goodies and who are the baddies.

JUNE

MONDAY 22
(173-192) WEEK 26
PAYE Week 12

TUESDAY 23
(174-191) WEEK 26

WEDNESDAY 24
(175-190) WEEK 26

Government Security enquiries are only used for 'killing' press stories. Their sole purpose is to enable the Prime Minister to stand up in the House and say 'we have held a full enquiry and there is no evidence to substantiate these charges!'

THURSDAY 25
(176-189) WEEK 26

FRIDAY **26**
(177-188) WEEK 26
● New Moon

SATURDAY **27**
(178-187) WEEK 26
sr 04.45, ss 21.22

SUNDAY **28**
(179-186) WEEK 26
2nd after Trinity

Note on European Identity Card: The F.O. is willing to go along with the idea as a quid pro quo for settlement over the butter mountain, the wine lake, the milk ocean, the lamb war and the cod stink.

Further note on European Identity Card: The Germans will love it, the French will ignore it, and the Italians and Irish will be too chaotic to enforce it. Only the British will carry it and resent it.

JUNE/JULY

MONDAY **29**
(180-185) WEEK 27
PAYE Week 13

Any document that removes the power of decision from Ministers and gives it to the Civil Service is important.

TUESDAY **30**
(181-184) WEEK 27

We must always have the right to promote the best man for the job regardless of sex.

WEDNESDAY **1**
(182-183) WEEK 27
Bank Holiday in Canada

THURSDAY **2**
(183-182) WEEK 27

FRIDAY **3**

(184-181) WEEK 27

Bank Holiday in USA

SATURDAY **4**

(185-180) WEEK 27

◐ First Quarter Independence Day, USA

sr 04.49, ss 21.20

SUNDAY **5**

(186-179) WEEK 27

3rd after Trinity

If you allow the principle of money being taken from the Arts and given to ordinary people to enjoy themselves, where will it end?

JULY

MONDAY 6
(187-178) WEEK 28
PAYE Week 14

TUESDAY 7
(188-177) WEEK 28

Open Government is rather like the live theatre: in order to have something you are prepared to show openly, there must first be much hidden activity.

WEDNESDAY 8
(189-176) WEEK 28

THURSDAY 9
(190-175) WEEK 28

Speeches are not written for the audience to which they are delivered. Delivering the speech is merely the formality that has to be gone through in order to get the press release into the newspapers.

FRIDAY **10**
(191-174) WEEK 28

SATURDAY **11**
(192-173) WEEK 28
○ Full Moon
sr 04.56, ss 21.16

The Civil Service generally hopes there'll be no movement on any subject.

SUNDAY **12**
(193-172) WEEK 28
4th after Trinity

JULY

MONDAY 13
(194-171) WEEK 29
Bank Holiday in N. Ireland
PAYE Week 15

TUESDAY 14
(195-170) WEEK 29

WEDNESDAY 15
(196-169) WEEK 29

It's not my job to care. That's what politicians are for. It's my job to carry out government policy.

THURSDAY 16
(197-168) WEEK 29

The public do not know anything about wasting public money. We are the experts.

JULY

FRIDAY 17
(198-167) WEEK 29
◑ Last Quarter

I am neither pro- or anti-anything.
I am merely a Humble Vessel
into which Ministers pour the
fruits of their deliberations.

SATURDAY 18
(199-166) WEEK 29
sr 05.04, ss 21.09

SUNDAY 19
(200-165) WEEK 29
5th after Trinity

JULY

MONDAY **20**
(201-164) WEEK 30
PAYE Week 16

When things go wrong, a Minister's first instinct is to rat on his department. A Civil Servant's first instinct is to rat on another department.

TUESDAY **21**
(202-163) WEEK 30

WEDNESDAY **22**
(203-162) WEEK 30

THURSDAY **23**
(204-161) WEEK 30

JULY

FRIDAY 24
(205-160) WEEK 30

SATURDAY 25
(206-159) WEEK 30
● New Moon
sr 05.13, ss 21.00

If we are to have a twenty-five per cent quota of women, we must have a much larger intake at the recruitment stage. So that eventually we'll have twenty-five per cent in the top jobs – in twenty-five years.

SUNDAY 26
(207-158) WEEK 30
6th after Trinity

Basic rules of Government:
1) Never look into anything you don't have to;
2) Never set up an enquiry unless you know in advance what its findings will be;
3) Never hold a meeting until you have written the minutes;
4) Never begin a conference until you have agreed the final communiqué;
5) Always write the conclusion before you look for the evidence.

JULY

MONDAY 27
(208-157) WEEK 31
PAYE Week 17

Every new Minister we have had would have been a laughing-stock within his first three weeks in office if it had not been for the most rigid and impenetrable secrecy about what he was up to.

TUESDAY 28
(209-156) WEEK 31

WEDNESDAY 29
(210-155) WEEK 31

THURSDAY 30
(211-154) WEEK 31

RESTRICTED means it was in the papers yesterday.
CONFIDENTIAL means it won't be in the papers till today.

FRIDAY **31**
(212-153) WEEK 31

SATURDAY **1**
(213-152) WEEK 31
sr 05.23, ss 20.50

SUNDAY **2**
(214-151) WEEK 31
◐ First Quarter
7th after Trinity

Law of Inverse Relevance: The less you intend to do about something the more you have to keep talking about it.

AUGUST

MONDAY 3
(215-150) WEEK 32
Bank Holiday in Scotland & Rep. of Ireland
PAYE Week 18

One never trusts anyone that one has deceived.

TUESDAY 4
(216-149) WEEK 32

WEDNESDAY 5
(217-148) WEEK 32

THURSDAY 6
(218-147) WEEK 32

Most of the really powerful offices in the world are called 'Secretary' – Cabinet Secretary, Secretary of State, Permanent Secretary, General Secretary etc. 'Secretary' means the person who is entrusted with the secrets, the information no one else knows.

AUGUST

FRIDAY 7
(219-146) WEEK 32

SATURDAY 8
(220-145) WEEK 32
sr 05.34, ss 20.38

SUNDAY 9
(221-144) WEEK 32
○ Full Moon
8th after Trinity

Note on internal enquiries: The job of a professionally conducted internal enquiry is to unearth a great mass of no evidence.

Note on full departmental enquiries: An even greater mass of no evidence is unearthed.

AUGUST

MONDAY **10**
(222-143) WEEK 33
PAYE Week 19

TUESDAY **11**
(223-142) WEEK 33

WEDNESDAY **12**
(224-141) WEEK 33

There are a number of issues
about which a Minister
automatically tells lies, and he
would be regarded as foolish or
incompetent if he told the truth.

THURSDAY **13**
(225-140) WEEK 33

FRIDAY **14**
(226-139) WEEK 33

SATURDAY **15**
(227-138) WEEK 33
sr 05.15, ss 20.24

No communiqué ever bears any relation to what you actually say. It's just a sort of visa. Gets you past the press corps.

SUNDAY **16**
(228-137) WEEK 33
◑ Last Quarter
9th after Trinity

Regional Arts Associations:

Art and local government go rather well together – the art of jiggery pokery.

AUGUST

MONDAY 17
(229-136) WEEK 34
PAYE Week 20

TUESDAY 18
(230-135) WEEK 34

The ordinary rules of living don't apply to Civil Servants: they don't suffer from unemployment, they automatically get honours, and inflation simply increases their pensions.

WEDNESDAY 19
(231-134) WEEK 34

Politicians are like children. You can't just give them what they want. It only encourages them.

THURSDAY 20
(232-133) WEEK 34

FRIDAY 21
(233-132) WEEK 34

SATURDAY 22
(234-131) WEEK 34
sr 05.56, ss 20.10

Subsidy is for Art. It is for Culture. It is not to be given for what people want. It is for what the people don't want but ought to have. If they really want something they will pay for it themselves.

SUNDAY 23
(235-130) WEEK 34
10th after Trinity

AUGUST

MONDAY 24
(236-129) WEEK 35
● New Moon
PAYE Week 21

The Prime Minister giveth – and the Prime Minister taketh away. Blessed be the name of the Prime Minister.

TUESDAY 25
(237-128) WEEK 35

WEDNESDAY 26
(238-127) WEEK 35

Government isn't about good and evil, it's only about order and chaos.

THURSDAY 27
(239-126) WEEK 35

FRIDAY 28
(240-125) WEEK 35

The Church of England is primarily a social organisation, not a religious one.

SATURDAY 29
(241-124) WEEK 35
sr 06.07, ss 19.55

SUNDAY 30
(242-123) WEEK 35
11th after Trinity

AUGUST/SEPTEMBER

MONDAY 31

(243-122) WEEK 36
Bank Holiday in UK (except Scotland)
PAYE Week 22

The Prime Minister does not know his ACAS from his NALGO.

TUESDAY 1

(244-121) WEEK 36
◐ First Quarter

WEDNESDAY 2

(245-120) WEEK 36

THURSDAY 3

(246-119) WEEK 36

Secrets: He that would keep a secret must keep it secret that he has a secret to keep.

FRIDAY 4

(247-118) WEEK 36

SATURDAY 5

(248-117) WEEK 36
sr 06.19, ss 19.39

SUNDAY 6

(249-116) WEEK 36
12th after Trinity

Bishops need to be the sort of chaps who speak properly and know which knife and fork to use. They are someone to look up to.

SEPTEMBER

MONDAY 7
(250-115) WEEK 37
○ Full Moon Labor Day, USA & Canada
PAYE Week 23

TUESDAY 8
(251-114) WEEK 37

WEDNESDAY 9
(252-113) WEEK 37

Open-minded as I am about foreigners what will the Greeks want out of the EEC? An olive mountain and a retsina lake.

THURSDAY 10
(253-112) WEEK 37

FRIDAY **11**
(254-111) WEEK 37

We do not admit that MI6 exists.

SATURDAY **12**
(255-110) WEEK 37
sr 06.30, ss 19.23

Brussels is full of hard-working public servants who have to endure a lot of exhausting travel and tedious entertainment.

SUNDAY **13**
(256-109) WEEK 37
13th after Trinity

SEPTEMBER

MONDAY **14**
(257-108) WEEK 38
PAYE Week 24

TUESDAY **15**
(258-107) WEEK 38
◑ Last Quarter

You cannot call Civil Service delays 'tactics'. That would be to mistake lethargy for strategy.

WEDNESDAY **16**
(259-106) WEEK 38

Information is currency among government drivers.

THURSDAY **17**
(260-105) WEEK 38

FRIDAY **18**
(261-104) WEEK 38

SATURDAY **19**
(262-103) WEEK 38
sr 06.41, ss 19.07

SUNDAY **20**
(263-102) WEEK 38
14th after Trinity

There is no point in the Cabinet questioning the Treasury. On the rare occasions when the Treasury understands the question, the Cabinet does not understand the answers.

SEPTEMBER

MONDAY
21

(264-101) WEEK 39

PAYE Week 25

TUESDAY
22

(265-100) WEEK 39

WEDNESDAY
23

(266-99) WEEK 39

● New Moon

THURSDAY
24

(267-98) WEEK 39

FRIDAY **25**
(268-97) WEEK 39

SATURDAY **26**
(269-96) WEEK 39
sr 06.52, ss 18.51

The Prime Minister doesn't think it's silly to appoint people who are vain and incompetent. Look at the Cabinet.

SUNDAY **27**
(270-95) WEEK 39
15th after Trinity

Questions of administrative policy can cause confusion between the administration of a policy and the policy of administration, especially when responsibility for the administration conflicts or overlaps with responsibility for the policy of the administration of the policy.

First law of political indiscretion: You always have a drink before you leak.

SEPTEMBER/OCTOBER

MONDAY **28**
(271-94) WEEK 40
PAYE Week 26

The Industry Secretary is the idlest man in town, the Education Secretary's illiterate and the Employment Secretary unemployable.

TUESDAY **29**
(272-93) WEEK 40

WEDNESDAY **30**
(273-92) WEEK 40
◐ First Quarter

THURSDAY **1**
(274-91) WEEK 40

OCTOBER

FRIDAY 2
(275-90) WEEK 40

SATURDAY 3
(276-89) WEEK 40
sr 07.04, ss 18.35

Women find top jobs very difficult. If you go around promoting women just because they are the best person for the job, you could cause a lot of resentment throughout the Civil Service.

SUNDAY 4
(277-88) WEEK 40
16th after Trinity

Civil Service standard reply when pressed for a straight answer: As far as we can see, looking at it by and large, taking one thing with another, then in the last analysis it is probably true to say, at the end of the day, you would find, in general terms that, not to put too fine a point on it, there really was not very much in it one way or the other.

OCTOBER

MONDAY 5
(278-87) WEEK 41
PAYE Week 27

TUESDAY 6
(279-86) WEEK 41

WEDNESDAY 7
(280-85) WEEK 41
○ Full Moon

There is no difference between
ends and means.

THURSDAY 8
(281-84) WEEK 41

OCTOBER

FRIDAY **9**
(282-83) WEEK 41

Most Government Departments achieve the opposite of their purpose: the Commonwealth Office lost us the Commonwealth, the Department of Industry reduces industry, the Department of Transport presided over the disintegration of our public transport system and the Treasury loses our money.

SATURDAY **10**
(283-82) WEEK 41
sr 07.15, ss 18.20

The Foreign Office aren't there to do things. They're there to explain why things can't be done.

SUNDAY **11**
(284-81) WEEK 41
17th after Trinity

OCTOBER

MONDAY 12
(285-80) WEEK 42
Columbus Day, USA Thanksgiving Day, Canada
PAYE Week 28

TUESDAY 13
(286-79) WEEK 42

One Prime Minister's lunch with an ambassador destroys two years of patient diplomacy.

WEDNESDAY 14
(287-78) WEEK 42
◑ Last Quarter

To a Minister, the word 'courageous' is even worse than 'controversial'. 'Controversial' only means it will lose you votes; 'courageous' means it will lose you the election.

THURSDAY 15
(288-77) WEEK 42

FRIDAY **16**
(289-76) WEEK 42

SATURDAY **17**
(290-75) WEEK 42
sr 07.27, ss 18.04

SUNDAY **18**
(291-74) WEEK 42
18th after Trinity

Presenting Proposals to Ministers:

1) Ministers will generally accept proposals which contain the words simple, quick, popular and cheap.
2) Ministers will generally throw out proposals which contain the words complicated, lengthy, expensive and controversial.
3) If you wish to describe a proposal in a way that guarantees that a Minister will reject it, describe it as courageous.

OCTOBER

MONDAY

19

(292-73) WEEK 43

PAYE Week 29

TUESDAY

20

(293-72) WEEK 43

Elevation from the House of Commons to the House of Lords is like being moved from the animals to the vegetables.

WEDNESDAY

21

(294-71) WEEK 43

THURSDAY

22

(295-70) WEEK 43

● New Moon

FRIDAY **23**
(296-69) WEEK 43

SATURDAY **24**
(297-68) WEEK 43
sr 07.39, ss 17.50

SUNDAY **25**
(298-67) WEEK 43
19th after Trinity
British Summertime ends

Reaction to speech by President of Buranda:
In practical terms we have the usual six options.
1) Do nothing.
2) Issue a statement deploring the speech.
3) Lodge an official protest.
4) Cut off aid.
5) Break off diplomatic relations.
6) Declare war.

Analysis of the six options:
1) If we do nothing we implicitly agree with the speech
2) If we issue a statement we just look foolish
3) If we lodge a protest it will be ignored
4) We can't cut off aid because we don't give any
5) If we break off diplomatic relations we cannot negotiate the oil rig contracts
6) If we declare war it might just look as if we were over-reacting.

OCTOBER

MONDAY **26**
(299-66) WEEK 44
Labor Day (New Zealand)
PAYE Week 30

It is instant ruin to be chairman of a nationalised industry. They might as well accept the golden handshake on the day they start. It's only a matter of time.

TUESDAY **27**
(300-65) WEEK 44

Practically everything that happens in government is suspicious.

WEDNESDAY **28**
(301-64) WEEK 44

THURSDAY **29**
(302-63) WEEK 44
◐ First Quarter

FRIDAY **30**
(303-62) WEEK 44

SATURDAY **31**
(304-61) WEEK 44
Hallowe'en
sr 06.51, ss 16.37

Official drivers are one of the most useful sources of information in Whitehall. Passengers forget that everything they say in the back seat can be overheard in the front.

SUNDAY **1**
(305-60) WEEK 44
20th after Trinity

NOVEMBER

MONDAY 2
(306-59) WEEK 45
PAYE Week 31

TUESDAY 3
(307-58) WEEK 45
Election Day, USA
Melbourne Cup Day

If the Prime Minister talks to underlings he may learn things that we don't know. Our whole position could be undermined.

WEDNESDAY 4
(308-57) WEEK 45

THURSDAY 5
(309-56) WEEK 45
O Full Moon

FRIDAY 6
(310-55) WEEK 45

SATURDAY 7
(311-54) WEEK 45
sr 07.04, ss 16.24

If a Minister is allowed to run his Department, the results are:

1) Chaos
2) Innovations
3) Public debate
4) Outside scrutiny.

SUNDAY 8
(312-53) WEEK 45
21st after Trinity
Remembrance Sunday

Essential Points on Reshuffles:
Ministers with a grip on the job are a nuisance because:

(a) They argue.
(b) They start to learn the facts.
(c) They ask if you have carried out instructions they gave you six months ago.
(d) If you tell them something is impossible they may dig out an old submission in which you said it was easy.

NOVEMBER

MONDAY 9

(313-52) WEEK 46
PAYE Week 32

TUESDAY 10

(314-51) WEEK 46

WEDNESDAY 11

(315-50) WEEK 46
Veterans' Day, USA
Remembrance Day, Canada

THURSDAY 12

(316-49) WEEK 46

Transport policy: This Department needs a transport policy like an aperture in the cranial cavity.

FRIDAY **13**
(317-48) WEEK 46
◑ Last Quarter

We are here to see that the Prime Minister is not confused. Politicians are simple people. They like simple choices. Clear guidance. They don't like doubt and conflict.

SATURDAY **14**
(318-47) WEEK 46
sr 07.18, ss 16.14

SUNDAY **15**
(319-46) WEEK 46
22nd after Trinity

The three articles of Civil Service faith:

1) It takes longer to do things quickly
2) It's more expensive to do things cheaply
3) It's more democratic to do things secretly

NOVEMBER

MONDAY **16**
(320-45) WEEK 47
PAYE Week 33

TUESDAY **17**
(321-44) WEEK 47

WEDNESDAY **18**
(322-43) WEEK 47

Civil Service Code (1):

I think we have to be very careful.
Translation: We are not going to do this.

THURSDAY **19**
(323-42) WEEK 47

FRIDAY **20**
(324-41) WEEK 47

Civil Service Code (2):

It is a slightly puzzling decision.
Translation: Minister, that is the silliest thing I have ever heard.

SATURDAY **21**
(325-40) WEEK 47
sr 07.28, ss 16.05
● New Moon

SUNDAY **22**
(326-39) WEEK 47
Last after Trinity

Standard Foreign Office Four-Stage Response to any crisis:

(1) Say nothing is going to happen.
(2) Say something may be going to happen, but we should do nothing about it.
(3) Say maybe we should do something about it, but there's nothing we can do.
(4) Say maybe there was something we could have done but it's too late now.

NOVEMBER

MONDAY **23**
(327-38) WEEK 48
PAYE Week 34

It is not necessary to let Ministers know what everybody else knows.

TUESDAY **24**
(328-37) WEEK 48

Public opinion is not yet ready for such a step. Meaning: public opinion is ready but the Civil Service is not.

WEDNESDAY **25**
(329-36) WEEK 48

THURSDAY **26**
(330-35) WEEK 48
Thanksgiving Day, USA

FRIDAY 27
(331-34) WEEK 48

SATURDAY 28
(332-33) WEEK 48
sr 07.39, ss 15.58
◐ First Quarter

SUNDAY 29
(333-32) WEEK 48
Advent Sunday

NOVEMBER/DECEMBER

MONDAY **30**
(334-31) WEEK 49
St. Andrew's Day
PAYE Week 35

Civil Service Code (3):

Have you thought through all the implications?
Translation: You are not going to do this.

TUESDAY **1**
(335-30) WEEK 49

WEDNESDAY **2**
(336-29) WEEK 49

THURSDAY **3**
(337-28) WEEK 49

DECEMBER

FRIDAY 4

(338-27) WEEK 49

Civil Service Code (4):

CGSM (Consignment of Geriatric Shoe Manufacturers).
Translation: A load of old cobblers.

SATURDAY 5

(339-26) WEEK 49
sr 07.49, ss 15.53
○ Full Moon

SUNDAY 6

(340-25) WEEK 49
2nd in Advent

DECEMBER

MONDAY 7
(341-24) WEEK 50
PAYE Week 36

TUESDAY 8
(342-23) WEEK 50

It's well known that social problems increase to occupy the total number of social workers available to deal with them.

WEDNESDAY 9
(343-22) WEEK 50

THURSDAY 10
(344-21) WEEK 50

The hypothetical example is an excellent way of deflecting attention from real problems.

DECEMBER

FRIDAY 11
(345-20) WEEK 50

Conventional forces are terribly expensive. Much cheaper just to press a button.

SATURDAY 12
(346-19) WEEK 50
sr 07.57, ss 15.52

SUNDAY 13
(347-18) WEEK 50
3rd in Advent
◑ Last Quarter

Bernard's ideas for slogans to make the Department more popular:
1) ADMINISTRATION SAVES THE NATION
2) RED TAPE IS FUN
3) RED TAPE HOLDS THE NATION TOGETHER.

DECEMBER

MONDAY 14
(348-17) WEEK 51
PAYE Week 37

TUESDAY 15
(349-16) WEEK 51

WEDNESDAY 16
(350-15) WEEK 51

The police have suffered an acute personnel establishment shortfall.
Translation: They are short-staffed.

THURSDAY 17
(351-14) WEEK 51

DECEMBER

FRIDAY 18
(352-13) WEEK 51

SATURDAY 19
(353-12) WEEK 51
sr 08.02, ss 15.53

SUNDAY 20
(354-11) WEEK 51
4th in Advent
● New Moon

DECEMBER

MONDAY **21**
(355-10) WEEK 52
PAYE Week 38

TUESDAY **22**
(356-9) WEEK 52
Shortest Day

WEDNESDAY **23**
(357-8) WEEK 52

THURSDAY **24**
(358-7) WEEK 52

Moral principles require the government to ban smoking. But when four billion pounds of revenue is at stake, we have to consider very seriously how far we are entitled to indulge ourselves in the rather selfish luxury of pursuing moral principles.

FRIDAY **25**
(359-6) WEEK 52
Christmas Day

SATURDAY **26**
(360-5) WEEK 52
sr 08.00, ss 15.56
Boxing Day

SUNDAY **27**
(361-4) WEEK 52
1st after Christmas
◐ First Quarter

Britain has had the same foreign policy objective for at least the last five hundred years – to create a disunited Europe. In that cause we have fought with the Dutch against the Spanish, with the Germans against the French, with the French and Italians against the Germans, and with the French against the Italians and Germans. In other words, divide and rule.

DECEMBER

MONDAY **28**
(362-3) WEEK 53
Bank Holiday in UK, Rep. of Ireland & Canada
PAYE Week 39

TUESDAY **29**
(363-2) WEEK 53

WEDNESDAY **30**
(364-1) WEEK 53

THURSDAY **31**
(365) WEEK 53

It is a curious fact that something that is wrong from every other point of view can be right politically.

JANUARY 1988

FRIDAY **1**
(1-365) WEEK 53
New Year's Day—
Bank Holiday in UK, Rep. of Ireland, Canada & USA

SATURDAY **2**
(2-364) WEEK 53

SUNDAY **3**
(3-363) WEEK 53
2nd after Christmas

ADDRESSES

BY APPOINTMENT TO HER MAJESTY THE QUEEN SUPPLIERS OF PROVISIONS AND HOUSEHOLD GOODS HARRODS LTD LONDON

BY APPOINTMENT TO H R H THE DUKE OF EDINBURGH OUTFITTERS HARRODS LTD LONDON

Harrods

HARRODS LIMITED
KNIGHTSBRIDGE LONDON SW1X 7XL

BY APPOINTMENT TO H M QUEEN ELIZABETH THE QUEEN MOTHER SUPPLIERS OF CHINA, GLASS AND FANCY GOODS HARRODS LTD LONDON

BY APPOINTMENT TO H R H THE PRINCE OF WALES OUTFITTERS AND SADDLERS HARRODS LTD LONDON

TELEPHONE 01-730 1234 TELEX 24319 FAX 01-581 0470 REGISTERED OFFICE 87/135 BROMPTON ROAD, LONDON SW1X 7XL REGISTERED IN LONDON NO 30209

17 March 1987

Sir Humphrey Appleby KCB
'Parnassus'
The Grove
Haslemere
Surrey

ANTIQUES

Antiquarius
135/141 King's Rd., SW3 (01) 351 5353
Bond Street Antique Centre
124 New Bond St., W1 (01) 493 1854
Chelsea Antique Market
245-253 King's Rd., SW3 (01) 352 5689
Chenil Galleries
181/183 King's Rd., SW3 (01) 351 5353
Grays Antique Market
58 Davies St., W1 (01) 629 7034
Mallett
40 New Bond St., W1 (01) 499 7411

BOOK SHOPS

Foyles
119 Charing Cross Rd., WC2 (01) 437 5660
Hatchards
187 Piccadilly, W1 (01) 437 3924
Truslove & Hanson
205 Sloane St., SW1 (01) 235 2128
Waterstone & Co Ltd
99 Old Brompton Rd., SW7 (01) 581 8522

DRY CLEANING & VALETING

Jeeves of Belgravia
10 Pont St., SW1 (01) 235 1011
Lilliman & Cox
34 Bruton Place, W1 (01) 629 4555

HAIRDRESSER

Geo F. Trumper
9 Curzon St., W1 (01) 499 1850

STATIONERY

Frank Smythson Ltd
54 New Bond St., W1 (01) 629 8558

TOILETRIES

Czech & Speake
39C Jermyn St., SW1 (01) 439 0216
J. Floris
89 Jermyn St., SW1 (01) 930 2885
Penhaligon's Ltd
41 Wellington St., WC2 (01) 836 2150

Cameo Stamp Centre,
75 The Strand, WC2
(01) 836 0997

Sotheran's,
2-5 Sackville St., W1
(01) 734 1150

SHOES

John Lobb, Bootmaker
9 St. James's St., SW1 (01) 930 3664
Trickers, Shoemakers
67 Jermyn St., SW1 (01) 930 6395

SHIRTS AND SUITS

James Drew
3 Burlington Arcade, W1 (01) 493 0714
Hawes and Curtis
2 Burlington Gdns., W1 (01) 493 3803
Hilditch & Key
73 Jermyn St., SW1 (01) 930 5336
Tommy Nutter
19 Savile Row, W1 (01) 734 0831
Turnbull & Asser
71-72 Jermyn St., SW1 (01) 930 0502

COUNTRY CLOTHES

Cordings
19 Piccadilly, W1 (01) 734 0834

STORES

Aquascutum
100 Regent St., W1 (01) 734 6090
Burberry's of London
165 Regent St., W1 (01) 734 4060
Harrods
Knightsbridge, SW1 (01) 730 1234
Liberty & Co Ltd
Regent St., W1 (01) 734 1234
Moss Bros
Bedford St., WC2 (01) 240 4567
Simpson (Piccadilly Limited)
Piccadilly, W1 (01) 734 2002

MUSIC

London Coliseum
St. Martin's Lane, WC2 (01) 836 3161
Royal Albert Hall
Kensington Gore, SW7 (01) 589 8212
Royal Festival Hall
Belvedere Rd., SE1 (01) 921 0600
Royal Opera House
Covent Garden, WC2 (01) 240 1200

Glyndebourne Festival Opera,
Lewes, E. Sussex
(0273) 812321

CARTE DU JOUR

RESTAURANTS

Antoine's
40 Charlotte St., W1 (01) 636 2817

Boulestin
25 Southampton St., WC2 (01) 836 7061

Café Royal
68 Regent St., W1 (01) 437 9090

Capital Hotel Restaurant
22-24 Basil St., SW3 (01) 589 5171

Carlton Tower Rib Room
Cadogan Place, SW1 (01) 235 5411

Connaught Restaurant,
Connaught Hotel
Carlos Place, W1 (01) 499 7070

Dorchester Grill Room
The Dorchester Hotel, Park Lane, W1
(01) 629 8888

Gay Hussar
2 Greek St., W1 (01) 437 0973

La Croisette
168 Ifield Rd., SW10 (01) 373 3694

La Tante Claire
68 Royal Hospital Rd., SW3 (01) 352 6045

Le Caprice
Arlington House, Arlington St., SW1
(01) 629 2239

Le Gavroche
43 Upper Brook St., W1 (01) 408 0881

L'Escargot
48 Greek St., W1 (01) 437 2679

Inigo Jones
14 Garrick St., WC2 (01) 836 6456

Langan's Brasserie
Stratton St., W1 (01) 493 6437

Leith's
92 Kensington Park Rd., W11 (01) 224 4481

Ma Cuisine
113 Walton St., SW3 (01) 584 7585

Mister Chow
151 Knightsbridge, SW7 (01) 589 7347

Mon Plaisir
21 Monmouth St., WC2 (01) 836 7243

Poon's of Covent Garden
41 King St., WC2 (01) 240 1743

The Ritz
Piccadilly, W1 (01) 493 8181

Rules
35 Maiden Lane, WC2 (01) 836 5314

Savoy Restaurant
Savoy Hotel, Strand, WC2 (01) 836 4343

Sheekey's
28 St. Martin's Ct., WC2 (01) 240 2565

Simpson in the Strand
100 Strand, WC2 (01) 836 9112

Sweetings
39 Queen Victoria St., EC4 (01) 248 3062

Tate Gallery Restaurant
Tate Gallery, Millbank, SW1 (01) 834 6754

Walton's
121 Walton St., SW3 (01) 584 0204

Wheeler's
19 Old Compton St., W1 (01) 437 2706

White Tower
1 Percy St., W1 (01) 636 8141

Gaylord,
16 Albermarle St., W1
(01) 629 9802

Bubbs,
329 Central Market, Smithfield,
EC1
(01) 236 2435

Locket's,
Marsham Court, Marsham St.,
SW1
(01) 834 9552

Massey's Chop House,
38 Beauchamp Place, SW3
(01) 589 4856

FOOD

Camisas (Italian)
1A Berwick St., W1 (01) 437 7120
Charbonnel et Walker (Chocolate)
24 Old Bond St., W1 (01) 629 4396
Cobb of Knightsbridge (Butcher)
5 Sloane St., SW1 (01) 235 5377
Fortnum & Mason Ltd
(General & Gourmet)
181 Piccadilly, W1 (01) 734 8040
Hobbs & Co (Gourmet)
29 South Audley St., W1 (01) 409 1058
Monmouth Coffee House
27 Monmouth St., WC2 (01) 836 5272
Patisserie Valerie (Cakes)
44 Old Compton St., W1 (01) 437 3466
Paxton & Whitfield (Cheese)
93 Jermyn St., SW1 (01) 930 9892
Richards (Soho) Ltd (Fishmonger)
11 Brewer St., W1 (01) 437 1358
The Tea House
15A Neal St., WC2 (01) 240 7539

WINES & SPIRITS

Grants of St. James's Ltd
Bury St., SW1 (01) 839 6886
Harveys of Bristol
12 Denmark St., Bristol 1 (0272) 83161
La Vigneronne
105 Old Brompton Rd., SW7 (01) 589 6113
Loeb & Co
15 Jermyn St., SW1 (01) 734 5878

The Hamper People of Norfolk,
Strumpshaw, Norfolk
(0603) 713937

Justin de Blank Provisions
(General & Gourmet)
42 Elizabeth St., SW1
(01) 730 0605

Berry Bros & Rudd,
3 St James's St., SW1
(01) 930 1888

FLOWERS

Moyses Stevens Ltd
6 Bruton St., W1 (01) 493 8171
Joan Palmer
31 Palmer St., SW1 (01) 222 4364
Pullbrook and Gould
181 Sloane St., SW1 (01) 235 3920

HATS

James Lock
6 St. James's St., SW1 (01) 930 5849
Herbert Johnson Ltd
18 Old Burlington St., W1 (01) 439 7397

PUBLICATIONS

Country Life
King's Reach Tower, Stamford St., SE1
(01) 261 7058
House and Garden
Vogue House, Hanover Sq., W1
(01) 499 9080
The Lady
38 & 40 Bedford St., WC2 (01) 836 8705
Punch
23-27 Tudor St., EC4 (01) 583 9199
Sporting Life
4 New Fetter Lane, EC4 (01) 353 0246

HOTELS

Brown's Hotel
Dover St., W1 (01) 493 6020
Claridges
Brook St., W1 (01) 629 8860
Ritz Hotel
Piccadilly, W1 (01) 493 8181
The Savoy Hotel
WC2 (01) 836 4343

CLUBS

Athenaeum Club
Pall Mall, SW1 (01) 930 4843
Garrick Club
Garrick St., WC2 (01) 836 1737
The Reform Club
104 Pall Mall, SW1 (01) 930 9374
Royal Automobile Club
89 Pall Mall, SW1 (01) 930 2345

The Flowersmith
34 Shelton St., WC2
(01) 240 6688

LIBRARIES

The British Museum Library
Gt. Russell St., WC1 (01) 636 1555
The London Library
14 St. James's Sq., SW1 (01) 930 7705

RACING

Ascot
Berkshire (0990) 22211
Cheltenham
Gloucestershire (0242) 523102
Epsom
Surrey (78) 26311
Fontwell Park
Sussex (0444) 50989
Goodwood
Sussex (0243) 774107
Kempton Park
Middlesex (76) 82292
Lingfield Park
Surrey (0342) 832009
Newbury
Berkshire (0632) 40015
Newmarket
Suffolk (0638) 4151
Plumpton
Sussex (0444) 50989

CRICKET

Lord's
St. John's Wood Rd., NW8 (01) 289 1615
The Oval
Kennington, SE1 (01) 735 4911

GOLF

Sunningdale Golf Club
Sunningdale, Berkshire (0990) 26064

TENNIS

Wimbledon All England Lawn Tennis & Croquet Club
Church Rd., SW19 (01) 946 2244
Queens Club
Palliser Rd., W14 (01) 385 3421

ESTATE AGENTS

Cluttons
74 Grosvenor St., W1 (01) 491 2768
Knight Frank & Rutley
152 Sloane St., SW1 (01) 730 8771
Savills
139 Sloane St., SW1 (01) 730 7152
Sturgis & Son
61 Park Lane, W1 (01) 493 1401

GIFTS

Asprey & Co Ltd
165 New Bond St., W1 (01) 493 6767
Alfred Dunhill
30 Duke St., SW1 (01) 499 9566
Garrard & Co Ltd
112 Regent St., W1 (01) 734 7020
The General Trading Company
144 Sloane St., SW1 (01) 730 0411
Halycon Days Ltd
105 New Bond St., W1 (01) 629 8811
Parrots
56 Fulham Rd., SW3 (01) 584 5699

GALLERIES

Hayward Gallery
Belvedere Rd., SE1 (01) 928 3144
National Gallery
Trafalgar Sq., WC2 (01) 839 3321
National Portrait Gallery
2 St. Martin's Pl., WC2 (01) 930 1552
Queen's Gallery
Buckingham Palace, Buckingham Palace Rd., SW1 (01) 930 4832
Royal Academy of Arts
Piccadilly, W1 (01) 734 9052
Tate Gallery
Millbank, SW1 (01) 821 1313
Wallace Collection
Manchester Sq., W1 (01) 935 0687

MUSEUMS

Apsley House
Hyde Park Corner, W1 (01) 499 5676
British Museum
Great Russell St., WC1 (01) 636 1555
Natural History Museum
Cromwell Rd., SW7 (01) 589 6323
Science Museum
Exhibition Rd., SW7 (01) 589 3456
Sir John Soane Museum
13 Lincoln's Inn Fields, WC2 (01) 405 2107
Victoria and Albert Museum
Cromwell Rd., SW7 (01) 589 6371

AUCTIONEERS

Bonhams
Montpelier Galleries, Montpelier St., SW7 (01) 584 9161
Christies
8 King St., SW1 (01) 839 9060
Phillips
7 Blenheim St., W1 (01) 629 6602
Sotheby's
34 New Bond St., W1 (01) 493 8080

ADDRESSES

Balliol College,
Oxford
(0865) 249601

ADDRESSES

NOTES

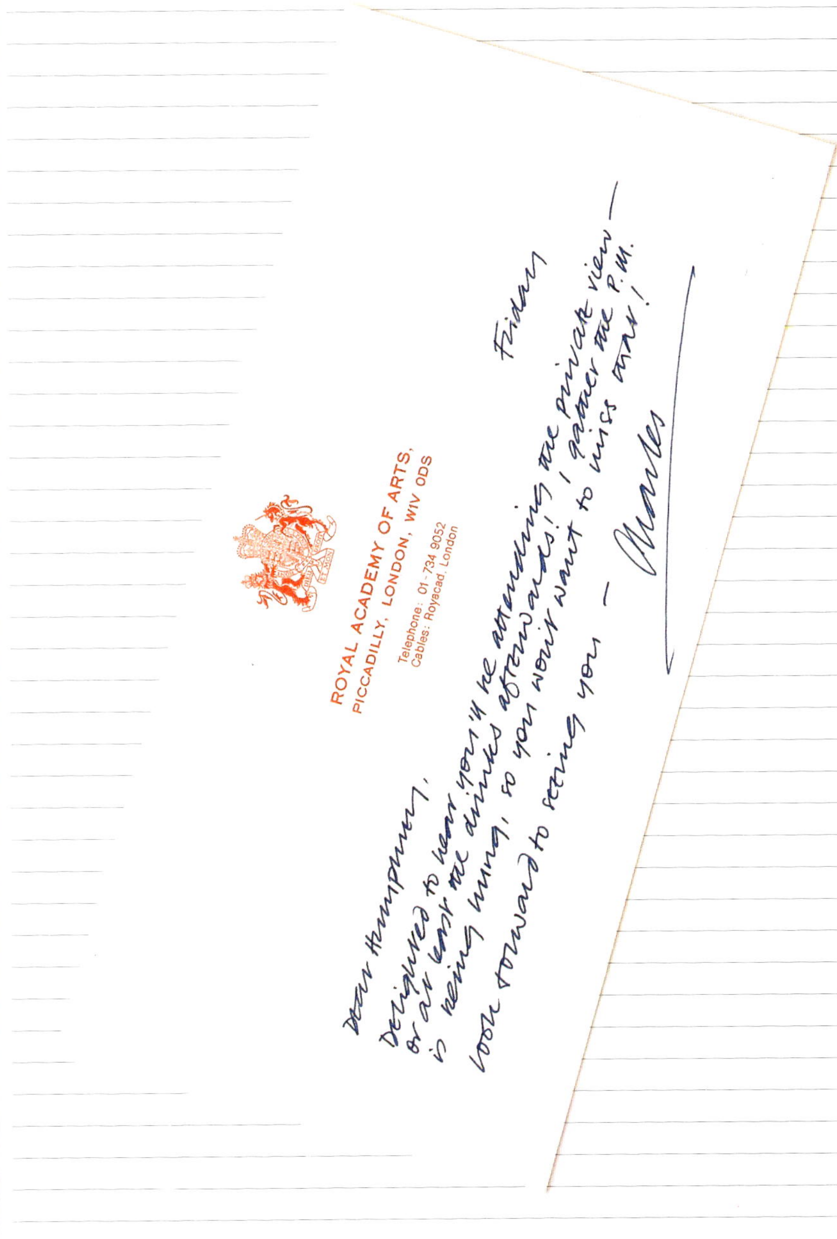
ROYAL ACADEMY OF ARTS,
PICCADILLY, LONDON, W1V 0DS

Telephone: 01-734 9052
Cables: Royacad, London

Friday

Dear Humphrey,

Delighted to hear you'll be attending the private view – or at least the drinks afterwards! I gather the P.M. is being hung, so you won't want to miss that!

Look forward to seeing you – Charles

NOTES

NOTES

NOTES